HOPE

For Digby, Dug, Buddy, Radnor
and their loving families – C.A.

To my favourite English girls, Aurèle and Caz.
Thanks to Sarah – S.P.

Quarto is the authority on a wide range of topics.

Quarto educates, entertains and enriches the lives of
our readers—enthusiasts and lovers of hands-on living.

www.quartoknows.com

© 2019 Quarto Publishing plc
Text © Corrinne Averiss
Illustrations © Sébastien Pelon

Corrinne Averiss has asserted her right to be identified as the author of this work.
Sébastien Pelon has asserted his right to be identified as the illustrator of this work.

First published in 2019 by words & pictures,
an imprint of The Quarto Group.
The Old Brewery, 6 Blundell Street,
London N7 9BH, United Kingdom.
T (0)20 7700 6700 F (0)20 7700 8066
www.QuartoKnows.com

A catalogue record for this book is available from the British Library.

ISBN: 978 0 71124 173 2

9 8 7 6 5 4 3 2 1

Manufactured in Shenzhen, China PP062019

HOPE

words & pictures

Comet was Finn's very best friend.
He loved to walk Finn to the park.

He loved to sit close by
when Finn played.

And best of all, he loved
to fall asleep in Finn's den.

But one day, Comet
wouldn't leave his bed.
Not for walks.
Not for trains.
Not even for a snooze
in Finn's den.

"He's poorly," said Mum,
"he needs to go to the vet's."

Finn wrapped Comet in his favourite blanket,
and Dad gently lifted him into the car.

"What's going to happen?" asked Finn.
"We will try to fix him," said the vet, gently.
"He might get better or he might get worse,
but we will look after him."

"Can I stay with him?" Finn asked Dad.

Dad shook his head.

At home, Finn crawled into his den.
He pulled down the flap so it was dark,
and his eyes filled with tears.

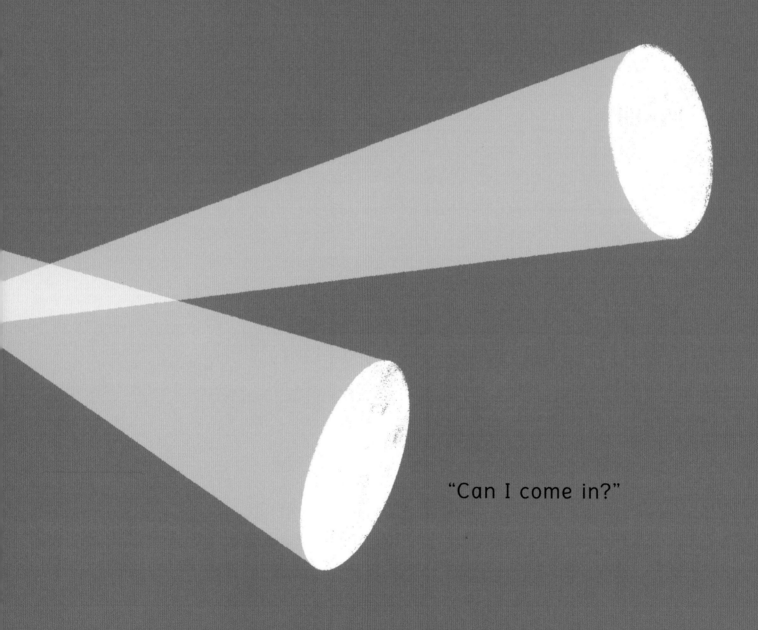

A little spot appeared on the wall!
It swirled around, then disappeared...

"Can I come in?"

It was Dad,
with a torch.

"You look sad," he said. "I feel sad too."

"What can we do?" sighed Finn.
"All we can do is hope." Dad gave the torch
to Finn. "Hope is keeping a little light on,
however dark things seem."

As Dad left the den,
Finn flicked off the torch –

and then on again.

Off, on, off, on.

Hoping wasn't easy.
But Finn would do anything
for Comet. So he kept
his little light *on*.

Through dinner, Finn hoped that Comet was feeling brave.

In the bath tub, he hoped that someone was scratching behind his ears, just the way he liked.

And at story time, he hoped that Comet would come home, feeling better than ever.

While he was hoping, things didn't seem so bad.
"I'm hoping hard," he told Dad, as he kissed him goodnight.
"I know," said Dad, "me too."

Finn couldn't sleep. He stared at his light on the wall. Suddenly it was joined by an even bigger light, coming in from his window...

The Moon!

Full and bright in the night sky!

Hope is keeping a light on, however dark things seem, he thought. "Thank you, Moon," he said. And he sent out his biggest hope yet...

The hope that Comet knew how much he loved him.

The more Finn hoped, the more lights he saw appearing in the sky. Until his eyes began to close, and he drifted off to sleep.

As Finn slept, his hopes twinkled with others
in the night sky. Big hopes and little hopes.
Old ones and new ones.

Light shimmered down on the vet's at the
other side of town. All the animals lay quiet
and still, as the hopes of their humans shone
through the windows to find them.

"WAKE UP, SLEEPY HEAD!" shouted Dad.
Finn jumped up and ran downstairs as fast
as he could. So fast, he slipped on the last
step and landed on his bottom!

On the floor in front of him
was Comet's bed. His favourite
blanket lay inside.

But where was Comet?
Had Dad returned without him?
Was he still poorly?

But then...

"WOOF!"
"COMET!"
Finn held him close.
"He's tired but so much better," said Mum.
"I hoped for you," said Finn,
"I hoped to the Moon and back!"

Comet was soon well enough
to walk to the park again.

The new tunnel was a huge success!

And Comet was even allowed
to snooze in the den...

...whenever he liked.